Joseph Ignatius Constantine Clarke

Mâlmôrda

A Metrical Romance

Joseph Ignatius Constantine Clarke

Mâlmôrda
A Metrical Romance

ISBN/EAN: 9783337346751

Printed in Europe, USA, Canada, Australia, Japan

Cover: Foto ©Andreas Hilbeck / pixelio.de

More available books at **www.hansebooks.com**

MÂLMÔRDA

A METRICAL ROMANCE

JOSEPH I. C. CLARKE

AUTHOR OF " ROBERT EMMET, A TRAGEDY OF IRISH HISTORY "

G. P. PUTNAM'S SONS

NEW YORK
27 West Twenty-third St.

LONDON
24 Bedford St., Strand

The Knickerbocker Press

1893

Electrotyped, Printed, and Bound by
The Knickerbocker Press, New York
G. P. Putnam's Sons

TO MY WIFE MARY,

MY BEST INSPIRATION IN LIFE AND LOVE,
REAL AND IDEAL.

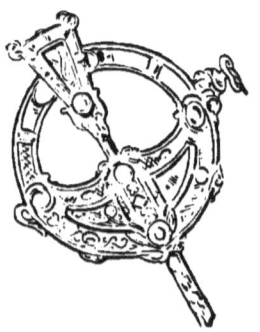

FORE-SONG.

—

To me by early morn
Came mem'ries of Old Ireland by the sea,
The tenderest and sweetest that there be,
Wherein the songs of water and of wind
And joy of loving human kind
Mingled in an ecstasy of harmony.
All was so low-toned and so sweet,
Near voices seeming ever to repeat
Soft syllables of blessing on my head ;
And the faces—ah, the faces of the dead
Companions of my youth were there,
And one face fairer than all faces fair,
And one face—oh, my mother—from whose eyes
The well-springs of all tendernesses rise ;
    And all were shaping
        Love and love and love !

II.

But at night again
Came the old, old pain,
And I saw the storm-gods whirling through the air,
With Desolation's armies ev'rywhere,
The long and lean lines, ragged, reaching back,
Torch-flared and wild-eyed in the wrack,
And the roll, roll, roll of the long thunder,
As the forked flash of the lightning leaped thereunder,
And nowhere any peace or rest
For the children of the land they called the Blest.
But the surges and the tempest loud were singing,
And the heavens through their wrath were with it ringing,
All shaping
Love and love and love !

III.

Oh my soul ! how can it be
That by still or stormy sea,
By the calm that swoons below, or the fury loose above,
The voice of Erin calls on love and love ?

Passionate our hearts be, well I know,
Whether our tears or laughter flow,
Whether our faces gloom or glow.
Yea, through our Irish souls Love's flame
Shoots its red blaze and shakes the frame ;
Beats on the heart with wings of fire,
As the wind's sleepless fingers shake a lyre,
Making wild eerie music never stilled.
And be our lives with toil or torment filled,
Ever a crisping, whisp'ring undertone,
Or hot-caught fiery breath makes known
The dominant, deep impulse that the hoar
Old ages stirred with, and that o'er and o'er
Re-born with travail in the hearts of men,
Is shaping on our lips, yea, now as then—
     Love and love and love !

IV.

    Then spake a voice to me :—
" Beyond the far days of the Flame-god's time
A fair god looked upon the young land's prime,
And on the mountains and the streams and seas

Set seals of loving.   Then in mystic threes
Came many gods to curse or bless,
Each with his portent of the soul's distress
Or rhapsody—Bravery, Envy, Jealousy,
Reverence, Pity, Faith—all joy that bides,
Or pain that lasts between the ocean's tides,
Or through the heaven-circling of a star.
All these have there endured to make or mar ;
But under the sea's breast ever stir the dreams
First waked by love, and in the babbling streams
Love murmurs all day long,
And down in the hearts of the mountains strong,
Love makes its melody of notes so deep
That the dead gods stir in their stony sleep,
        Their cold lips shaping
            Love and love and love ! "

                        v.

        Then full voiced came my song.
"Twixt day and dark the dead Past called to me.
A long wave rolled along the Irish sea,
Its white foam fronted with tossing spears,

Red with the rust of a thousand years.
It brake on the sands and the waters ran
With a blood-red stain, and the song began.
They were there, the steel-capped Ostman hordes;
In the dusk they flashed their two-edged swords.
Their warships tossed on the purpling waves ;
At the rowers' benches toiled the slaves.
Then the Irish king in his youth and might,
With sweep of battle and roar of fight
About him, and circling his Norseland prize,
The blue of the sea in her wild, sweet eyes,
The life of a man in each strand of her hair,
And the glow of a flame on her bosom bare.
'Mid storm and battle, by moon and mist,
I saw through their very souls, I wiste !
And the shields that rang, and the sobs that died,
And the echoing hills and the sombre tide
    Ever were shaping
        Love and love and love !

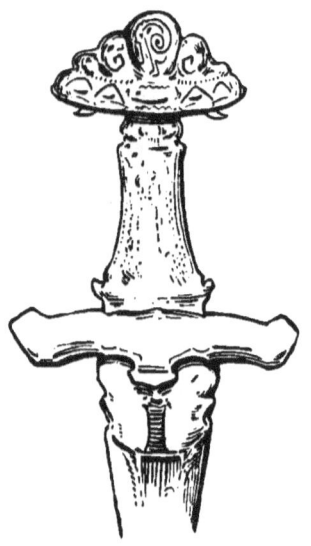

6

MALMORDA.

WHAT Gaelic chief dares thus to stand in arms
    Between th' encircling mountains and the sea ?
Hold not the Ostmen lordship o'er the land
That, like a cup of carven emerald,
Seems tilted to the waters blue from Brea
Unto Ben Edar ?

> Keen of sight and sharp
Of sword, and quick to strike these Danes ; but all
Their Southern watch, three hundred strong, went
   through
The woods of Shanganah ere break of dawn,
Led by a grizzled horseman, whose brown face,
Deep-seamed, of life-long battle told with waves
And winds and arméd men.
>   Woe to the Gael
When Asculp southward rides !
>   Woe to the Gall
When young Mâlmôrda, of Hy-Cualan king,
His mighty ax upraised leads on his kernes !
And 't is Mâlmôrda who from horse dismounts,
And up the hill beside his henchman strides,
As much at ease as though he trod the steeps
Of Doon.   His quick, free glance sweeps round ; he
   laughs
And with the tossing of his head his long
Black hair is shaken on the wind, its ringlets
Crisping o'er the woven bronze rings of his coat
Of mail.

A white cloud, westward rimmed with gold,
Hangs o'er the bay ; a summer drowse hangs o'er
The land, save for sharp clinkings from the woods
Beyond, or note of curlew from the sea.
Brief is Mâlmôrda's glance toward far Duv-linn
Where bides the Ostman strength behind thick walls,
And but a passing frown tells he has seen
A dark ship lab'ring past Ben Edar's head,
The sail scarce flapping, but two rows of oars
Rising and dipping on the pulsing waves ;
But when atow'rd the sweep of hills he turns,
Then stands he tall and masterful and points
With gesture sudden tow'rd the cloven mount,
And all his soul does battle in his eyes
Of steely gray.   A muttered something parts
The henchman's lips, whereat the chieftain, wroth,
Striking his ax-point in the turf, breaks forth :—

" Art thou my clansman, Angus ?   Set thy face
Against the cloudy reddening of the sun :
Thy keen eyes fix upon the hill-top dark

And base thought of Mâlmôrda harbor not.
I watched thee frowning thy thick brows as we
Pressed past Slieve Tual by the glen's deep woods,
Thy wolf-sharp glances sidewise shot as though
Thou fearedst my purpose.   Man, 't was not for thee
To judge thy battle-lord, e'en though I turned
From Cualan's hills, well knowing that the Gall
Was there to ravage if he durst.   Know then
Mâlmôrda with the Heathen palters not,
And makes no pact ; but stands on Ostman ground,
Betwixt him and Duv-linn, yea, at the gate
Of his home-coming, ready to send him fierce
God-blessings waved from sacramental swords.

" That likest thou better, so for Asculp watch—
The gray old pirate with the arm of steel—
And quick as thou seest their swarming helmets glint
Through the black frontage of the trees, raise thou
The Brann tribe's war-note on thy battle horn
Until the hills reply.   Our ambushed kernes
At battle sign shall charge on Asculp's flank,
While thou and I will lead in whelming charge

Our gallowglasses front-straight to the fray.
Too oft we 've sought to trap him and his Danes
Within our borders, but to find him steal
Back to his fortress lair by other ways.
Now well we know he dares not force Glen Doon
With his three hundred scant, and so must fare
Or West, or creep back North ; but North or West
His home trail leads him hither to our spears.
Dhar Dhia ! Angus, I am here to slay,
To slay gray Asculp as a Gall, a Dane,
A pirate fiend, wild sea-wolf, torturer,
Norse-demon, chartered by his dwarf gods four
To sail the main, to plunder, burn and kill—
All these fair titles to a bloody grave,
But for mine ax-blade stancher title yet,
He is the husband of my Torcala.

" Start not and lower that I 've named her name.
God sends us glories that we garner not,
For some small thing we blindly call their bane,
Which may be half their worth did we but know
It all. That she is pagan is enough

T' outweigh, for thee and those who set strong faith
Above strong love, all that her stormy gods
Have poured aplenty on her. Yet if I,
In penance for my sins and hers, but bring
Her o'er and lay her at the feet of Christ,
Shall not her beauty and her glory rise
A ray to Heaven and a joy to earth,
Fairer, as Christ said, that she 's won from hell?

" These fine thoughts trouble me, but ever lift
Their pointing fingers and their asking eyes
When bides she not by me. So, Angus, watch
While I in limnings rude trace out the tale,
Gazing, for help therein, upon the sea,—
Blue as the deeps are of her sea-blue eyes,
Deep as the ocean of the love that heaves
Beneath her bosom with great tides and storms
And after-swoons of calm—a calm wherein
My soul is borne thro' lumined caves where all
The wonders of the mystic world lie bare,
Seen in green crystal light. No sorceress,
I think not, but a woman fashioned fair
By great-brained artist gods.

" She was my prize.
Straight Irish skein to Ostman sword it was,
And my arm was the stronger that glad night
Of storm when Sitric's mighty fleet was scattered.

" Through the swift darkling eve we 'd stood agaze
Upon the outspread bay, our glances fixed
Where, startled by the swift in-sweeping storm,
The Ostmen ships were shifting restlessly,
Some standing out against the east wind's roar

As they would, past Ben Edar's misty head,
Face the mad menace of the Irish sea,
Which swirled, all lashed and whitened into foam,
Clapping its lusty hands in glee around them ;
While others heeled and tumbled as they ran
For shelter to the dykes at Liffie's mouth,
Since none dare turn to gain Delginis' Sound.
But one we saw, the huge ship of their king,
The golden dragon at her prow, and she
Broad-breasted, tugging at her anchor ropes
As though she trusted in her oaken ribs
And in her raven gods to split the wind
That roared in thunder-gusts upon her prow.
Oh, how we prayed their storm maids in the clouds,
That like to hissing whips their gray locks long
Outstreaming, they would shake along the sea,
And cast her loose in spite of churning oars
And reefed sail set aslant to ease the strain.
Rolled she thus there alone, the last and greatest
Of the swarming fleet as though she scorned to flee.

" At last, as o'er the frowning hills the sun
Went out in watery parting, and the lift

Grew sudden black, we saw by one sharp flash
The great hull drifting broadside to the waves.
Then knew we that the storm prevailed and she
Was ours, and surer ours the more they sweated
Trying to bring her beaten head around.
So poured we swarming down the steep to where
Above Delginis well we knew the waves
Would thrust and hold her fast. Then from the rocks
We saw her huge bulk looming, and her line
Of bulwark war-shields catching the white glint
Of foam, and rattling to the threshing sea.
On with the send of it the great ship came,
Her torn sail lashing at the mast ; her long
Oars splintering and crackling, when with crash,
As from a live thing's agony, her hull
Plunged, rending her stout timbers, plank and rib,
On Ireland's weed-hung granite, toothed for such
As she.
　　　Straight as she struck we leaped aboard,
Up clambering and smiting with our swords.
High on the poop stood Sitric Ravenhair,
The king, his golden helmet glittering.

2

On him I bent, and as he snatched a sword,
I plunged my short skein hilt-home in his neck.
Before he could on Thor or Odin call,
The Valkyrs had his spirit on their wings.
Heigh ! 't was rough work, the Ostmen rallying,
But still beat down upon the slippery deck,
The storm ahowl, the timbers crushing in,
Death cries and war cries mingled and the gleam
Of weapons in the levin flashing red.
Sudden a giant wave took up the ship
And planted her as in a granite jaw
Upon the shore.   Then was hot slaughter done.
Ours were they, and the plunder fever broke—
A rush for soldier trophies and rich spoils.

" Down under deck, among the dead I groped
To where I knew the cabin of the king
Must be, and first brake in.   Mine eyes grew large.
There in a royal chamber hung with silk,
And heaped with down-soft rugs, I saw a foe
My thought had never dreamed.   A woman 't was,
And oh ! for all the gold of the Ard Righ,

For all the pearls of all the sea maids fair,
I would not barter that first glance on her.
Against the silken curtains standing out,
Whose gathered folds she grasped with firm right hand,
Her lithe, ripe form in shimmery, clinging white
Rose queenlike, and her red-gold hair fell waved
About her neck and o'er her half-hid breast ;
But most her eyes that blue to violet burned
Did fix me.   Wide they glared, not terror-lit
Nor flaming in defiance, but in question.
She saw my sword gore-dripping and her glance
Said, 'Whose ?'   I answered, 'Sitric's,' and she said
In clearest speech, 'Not Asculp's ?'   'Lady, no,'
I said.   She shook the glory of her hair,
With what wild thought I knew not in her brain,
Half smiled, and then, as if to be resolved,
Again made question, 'Sitric's ?   Thou art sure ?'
'Ay, Sitric's,' said I in their Ostman speech,
'Art thou his queen ?'
                    'No, no, I 'm Asculp's wife,
Hast slain him ?'
                    Swam piteous now her eyes,

And toward me she extended her white arms.
'Was he aboard ?   If so he 's with the dead,'
I grimly answered as I forward strode.
She shrank back eying me with watchful glance
That of a sudden shot to malice keen :
'Were he aboard, thou hadst not trodden here ! '
I laughed, and springing to her side clutched fast
Her wrist.

   ' Thou art my spoil, and would thy lord
Were here to fight for thee ; thou 'rt worth the while.'
Above the clamor of the sea the clash
Of weapons came and fighting cries.   I loosed
My grasp, and saw her glance upon the marks
My crimsoned fingers made ; then quick she clutched
A heavy sword that hung upon a rack
And cried :—

    ' Heil, Asculp ! help me ! Asculp, here ! '
' An it be Asculp, lord of thee, he 's mine,'
I cried, and to the curtained door sprang fast.
A man fell bleeding at my feet—a Dane—
And died there with a groan, while after him
There came a press of Irish kernes who swung

Their skeins.

      ' Back, ev'ry man ; here is my spoil ;
The rest is for you all,' I cried and turned,
Grasping the proud white woman by the waist,
Then waved them off with threatening of my sword.
As went they sullenly, I felt her bend
To peer as with knit brows above the corse
That outstretched lay, the long gray beard
Blood-smeared.

      ' Not Asculp,' said she, and the smile
Came back to her that I had seen before.
Then writhed she from me, and with gesture quick,
Touching her brow, gazed sidewise at my face,
As if remembering something weird and charged
With fate.

      Ere morn, my kernes and I had stripped
The great ship of her bravery. The king's
Gold-graven helmet and his raven flag,
Great stores of arms, stout casks of wine, rich stuffs
From far off East, and little casks of gold.
A rich prize 't was, and when with heavy loads
Our soldiers toiled up Leinin's hill, we saw

The royal ship ablaze and lighting up
The heavens like a new fierce Irish dawn.
It gave me joy.   I turned to sate mine eyes
Withal, and felt as did our Druids old
Who welcomed thus the sun-god from the east
With fire before Lord Patrick came with mild,
Sweet Christ.   Beside me rested Torcala,
For whom a litter I had made, by stout
Kernes borne.   She gazed upon the burning ship,
When, sudden, a swift glitter in her eye
Told she had something seen that stirred her soul.
And there upon the rocks we had but left,
I saw, red-gleaming in the glare, a Dane,
Erect, his silvery beard fire-glorified,
His arm upraised as in a curse or prayer.

" ' 'T is Asculp !' cried I, looking in her eyes.
She bent her head.

      ' 'T is Asculp shorn of all,
His king, his ship, his sailors and his bride,
Most pitiable man !'

       ' Thy Lord,' I cried,

And drew again my blade ; but she clung hard
Upon my arm and said :—

                ' Hast not enough ?
All he has lost is thine, or else to thee
A glory.'

        But I pulled me free and said :—
' Let him lose truly all then with his life ! '
Whereat she flung herself upon the stones—
' Kill me the first, then.'   And she clutched a sword
From out the girdle of a gallowglass,
And handing me the hilt threw back her head,
Her white neck baring to the blow.

                   When next
I turned, lo ! the grim fire-lit form was gone
As swallowed in the gloom or by the sea.

" We went our way in silence, Torcala
Half-swooning as it seemed, but still to me
The half-smile I had seen aglimmering faint
About her lips and o'er the lashes long
That veiled her sea-deep eyes.

                Soon told she me

That Asculp had gone shoreward from the fleet,
For what she knew not, ere the storm arose;
That Sitric watched and waited him until
Too late to save the ship.
                  I saw it all.
He had been sent to spy the land, and deep
I cursed the moment I 'd let pass to hunt
So fell a foe to earth.
              Ah, Angus, there
In truth I erred.   If there be one weak spot
In Gaelic natures, it is where the will
Spurs not a purpose sword-straight to its goal,
But lets us stop short by a single step,
If but appeal be made unto our pride,
Yea, or our pity.   This I knew that day,
And ever since its warning beacon shines
To make me liker to our Ostmen foes.
'T is why I 'm here to-day to pay, though late,
The price, grim Angus, of my mercy then.
But other cause have I, as I 'll unfold.
Thou startest, Angus ; have thine eyes seen aught
Of Ostman helm or pennon in the pass?

A single kerne, light-footed, speeding him
As though he brings great news.
                      ' What is it, knave ? ' "

The wild kerne, spent with speed, leans on his spear,
And in hot gushes of his breath and with
Loose gesture backward to the hills, cries out :—
" The Ostman force is marching through the Skealp
And not a Gael to hinder !"
                     " Through the Skealp?
Well, well, how many ? "
                     " Scant two hundred men.
Had thy force, thrice their number, met them there
Not one had left the gray jaws of the hills
Alive."
           "And, clansman, why not here the same
Doom clip them ? "

                  " Ay, but at a bloodier cost."
Grim Angus grumbles, as his eyes flash fire.
" Who takes a bond of doom counts not the cost."
Swift flashes back Mâlmôrda, and then turns
Upon the kerne with rain of questioning.

He had but seen them from his eyrie high
As they into the pass pushed warily :
They had seen fight—that much was sure : they bore
Some wounded, and they drove some prisoners :
Most like their fight had been by Fercualan

    With old Lord Fallan, and had risked the
        pass
    Rather than try to force the shoreward trail.
    So might it be.

              At this Mâlmórda grasps
             With lighting of his face.
                " It must be so,
          Thou hast done bravely and
                hast shrewdly guessed;
          Shalt have a Danish thumb-
              ring for thy pains,

By full a league thou lead'st them ? Good ! A league 's
An hour for them, thus marching and thus cumbered.
Go, bid young Niall in the woods below,
Lie close behind the hazel trees until
The trumpet sounds ; then charge them, steel to steel.

The kerne is turning, all his face asmile
In joy of battle coming and reward
Made sure, mixed with brave worship of his chief,
Who tow'rs above him, royal, masterful,
When Angus halts him thus :—
       " Thou knowest not
For sure the prisoners were Fallan's men ? "
Mâlmôrda frowns ; the kerne slow answers, " No,"
And turns again. Mâlmôrda bites his lip.
" Now ask him," Angus saith, "what lieth next
Thy soul."
    The kerne stands wonder-eyed as strides
Tall Angus seven paces off and peers
Up to the hills, Mâlmôrda's eyes still bent
On him.
   " The shaggy war-dog loves me well.
He would not leave one doubt rest unresolved,
Yet, knowing that it tells no whit on what
We have in hand, would have me know 't alone.
Or fears he still—— ? " so in his beard Mâlmôrda
Mutters ; then to the kerne :—
       " Now quickly tell,

Did'st note a woman's robe among the Danes?
Thou know'st—thou would'st have known far off—her
    robe—
The robe of Lady Torcala, the fair
Silk robe of many dyes?"

                   "She was not there;
I looked for her," the kerne makes answer blunt,
As though he had of one he loved not spoken.
Mâlmôrda noted not the tone; the word
For him was all.

             "Go, soldier, clear of sight:
Come, Angus, come; she was not there. Thy doubts
Were mists; we 'll cleave through all of them before
The stars are out; an hour will tell it all.
An hour, old Asculp, till thy ravens feed!

"Angus, my kinsman, since we respite have,
I 'll tell thee something sacred under seal
That by St. Patrick's shrine thou 'lt keep it safe
Within thy breast till I am dead and thou
About to die!

" 'T is touching this fair Dane.
Thou 'lt keep thine oath.   We do not swear the man
We doubt or trust being sworn ; but thou hast loved
Me in thy grim, fierce way, and held me worth
Thy trust though all the rank growth of the clans,
Yea, our clan, has but growled and looked at me
Askance since that wild, clearing morn I brought
Her home.

   " Great was their joy through all the vales
At that great booty, and remember I
Full well how thou, fresh come from Temora,
So grumbledst that in taking Sitric's ship
Thou hadst no hand.

    " My joy was Torcala,
The beautiful, the wonderful, the queen
Of knowledge and of sorcery so sweet,
My soul swoons at the thought of it.   I loved ;
She loved, and all her wondrous tale she told,
Locked in mine arms within my castle keep :—
How she was born a Norseland viking's child ;

Her father made her gray old Asculp's wife,
Who ever loved her dotingly and heaped
All tenderness and kindness on her head.
But him she never loved save as a father ;
His heart was in his ship, and nights and days
To him were weary when they brought no fight
With men or waves ; and never was he gay,
Save when, a burning castle on his lee,
He steered away with plunder which he laid
With laughter at her feet.   She sailed with him
In wintry seas and under summer suns,
Plundering from Alba to the Spanish coast,
And once went through the pillars of the Straits
Upon a day of calm, his oarsmen toiling
While the hot sun blazed.   Then by Morocco's shore
They sailed and grappled with the Moslem there,
Winning great stores of finery.   At last,
Returned to Norway, Sitric Ravenhair,
The king I slew, made Asculp Admiral,
And with his fleet sailed hither to take fee
Of Harek who is Duv-linn's Ostman lord.
Thou knowest the rest of that.

"Her hands in mine—
Oh, such white hands and small and dainty shaped ! —
She told me how King Sitric had cast love
Before her, but she spurned such trait'rous wooing.
Yea, when she knew 't was his blood stained my sword,
Did she not strangely smile as I have told thee.
Old Asculp wished she safe from hurt because
His strong arm had upheld her ; but to me
She came, she said, a captive heart and soul.
Angus, there is a weird, strange tale in that.

"Her chamber in my keep she had arrayed
With trappings from the cabin of the ship.
The perfumed lamps, a spoil from Araby,
The rugs of glowing tint, the silken flags,
Small chimes of silver bells from Spain that rang
At laughter of the wind.   There stretched at length
She told me how she 'd learned soft Southern moods
For dreaming life away, and wished me so
To dream long whiles beside her ; then, strange ways
Of pagan love she taught me, passionate
Beyond a Christian's dream, as how to make

A love word linger on the lips, and live
Unspoken in the eyes and be renewed
Upon the finger tips in playing lute-like
On a lover's neck, until the whole frame
Thrilled like a stricken string. Then would she wind
Her fair white arms around me, and her soul
Would swoon within her. Often, springing up,
I 'd fly from her at night and roam along
The wind-swept hills, or hurry to the sea,
And plunge therein to dash her charms away.
But I 'd return full soon, mayhap to find
Her at the dawn, new-clad in shimm'ry robes,
Through which her warm flesh faintly showed its white,
Fast by her chamber window, drinking in
The freshness of the morn. Then would she be
The Norse-child, all her langour gone, her eyes
A sparkle, and her red-gold hair bound up.
Then would she sing me old Walhalla rhymes,
Or at my feet sit telling me weird things
The skalds had taught her. How the wonder-flame,
Halogi, rose—a giant golden fount—
Amid the ancient Night where was no world :

Then all the conflict between frost and fire,
And strange begettings of the melting ice,
And how the giants slew their sire, and made
The mountains of his bones, and of his blood
The seas, and of his skull the archéd heavens,
Setting their dwarf gods four, North, East, South, West,
At its four corners. Thereupon, I 'd laugh
And clip her to me, but she 'd whirl away
And, standing angered like a goddess, say
The Norns were by and would make strict account
Of any slight on Odin. Beautiful
She glowed then, telling me of Uri old,
Verdandi strong, and Skuld the young, the three
Fair women who were watching mortal men,
As we say angels watch us, and record
Our good and ill.

                "Often on moonlight nights
We wandered, hand in hand, along the hills
When all the air she peopled with her elves,
And unto every bush and rock and tree
She gave a fairy, and the nightingale

3

To her a spirit was of one who loved
As we loved, and whose song told endless bliss
That Death had no command upon.

                                   " But oh,
'T was by the sea, the sea-king's child made fast
Her hold upon me. There, where the waves broke
On the shingly stones, flooding and moving them
With plashing rush and rumble, would she stand,
And with her hair sent tossing by the wind,
Tell me with outspread arms of all the fleets
That battled with the storms where icebergs groaned
In livelong grinding of their glittering sides ;
Of sea-gods and sea-maidens who kept watch
For Odin's children, yet who sometimes lured
Great vessels to their doom. She knew the gods,
She said, but not their ways to men. It was
A riddle whose dark answer failed to come,
We meanwhile, driving on in blindness. 'T was
Not right to blame the gods for this ; they must
Have joys as men have, some in loving, some
In slaying. Logi laughed at evil wrought ;

Baldur, the Beautiful, both loved and smiled,
But the All-Father's face no man did know,
So far his shoulders rose above the skies ;
And if his eyelids ever oped or closed
In pity or in joy, they knew not sure.
Once, rapt thus, gazing out upon the moon
Just raising her full shield above the sea,
The trembling silver pathway at our feet
Breaking in silver melody, she laughed,
And, turning, twined her arms about my neck,
Looked a short instant in my face, and said,—
' I 'll tell it thee.   Thou art my love, and I
Am thine ; Is 't so ? '

                  For answer I but kissed
Her on her brow.

             ' It is a dream I 'll tell,
And dreams are kisses from the gods.   The night
Before our watchman on the mast cried, " Land ! "
Meaning this land of Erin, I lay down
To sleep, my mind thrilled with the talk between
King Sitric and my lord, about the kings
Of Erin, their stature tall, their might in war,

Untaught for most part in the deep device
Of warring, but as brave as mountain bears
That scarce knew what a wound meant, and their land
So fertile, and so fair its vales and woods.
I slept, and Beltsa, giant goddess, kissed
Mine eyes.   At first a mist and then a hill
I saw, and on it stood a towering man,
Long-haired and helmeted, with laughing eyes,
Whose right hand lifted up a bloody sword.
Whose blood so reddened it, I marvelled much,
Yet felt I knew ; but straight forgetting it,
As in our dreams we let our deep thoughts glide,
I fixed my gaze again upon his face.
A turmoil on the deck aroused me then.
Quick passed the dream.   'T was morn, the sun was up.
I flung a mantle round me, speeding forth,
And all green Erin's glory rose in joy
Before me.   Oh, what rhapsody took up
My soul in that first glance on gracious Erin.
Its rings of swelling hills that heaved in waves
Of sunlit emerald, and kissed the blue,
Fleece-flecked above, and met the blue

Foam-rimmed below ! " Ireland, sunland, joy-land ! "
Cried I in ecstasy, " thy headlands, curved
Like wide-embracing arms, stretch boldly out
Inviting me to lodge my head upon
Thy breast !" 'T was grand. E'en Asculp shouted
   " Heil ! "
And all the crew yelled with him.

                     " ' One green hill
I saw, and knew the hill-top of my dream,
Then prayed to Beltsa that the glad young king
Should stand there as the vision gave him shape.
The splashing of the anchors dashed my dream
To spray.   I turned to see King Sitric's fleet
Come sweeping after us like sea-gulls white,
In twos and threes until the sixty sail
Lay seaward ranged anear us, to await
Jarl Asculp's signal whether they should on
To Duv-linn bear or seek Delginis haven.
Why 't was in doubt I know not, save that 't was,
And Asculp launching a small boat with two
Stout rowers, made for shore.   The morn-lit land

Seen closer, fairer rose ; its
    sweeps of vale
Aglow with sunny tints that merged
    from pale
Corn-gold to yew-tree green ; the lime-white villages,
And, oh, the mountains like to woman's breasts,
Soft-rounded and slow heaving in their green
That distance deepened into steely blue
Against the warm blue sky.   Long leaned I gazing,
Our great ship " Raven of the Wind " arock
Upon the water, gently as a maid's
Heart beats ere love has raised its welcome storm,
While, like impatient hounds, the small craft tossed,
Their oarsmen keeping a slow stroke to hold
Them ready to hoist sail again, while ours,
Ten twelves of oars, stood in the waist and watched
King Sitric in his golden helmet fret,

As gazed he landward for a sign.   None came
He looked for.   And so, frowning dark, he strode
From 'mong his berserks at the prow and stood
Beside me, asking me with clenching hands
If sure Jarl Asculp was his friend or no.
Then blew a chilly breeze off shore, and quick
The sky grew gray, then slowly lowered to black.
A savage wind came roaring in from sea,
Whitening the water, while the headlands turned
To purple, and I felt their iron hands
Beneath the waves drag at our anchor ropes
Until we swung adrift, with mist and night
And storm around us.   Great were the cries,
The rush to oars, hoisting and wearing sail,
Sitric, a raving demon at the prow.
I saw the breakers tumbling on our lee,
And wet and wild-eyed went from deck below
To die, if so the Norns said in their wrath,
As should a viking's child.   When in the crash
And murder that came then, I saw thee spring
All drenched and bloody through the cabin door
I knew thee straight.   Thou wert mine Irish king,

And first it seemed to me I had not waked,
So fell to asking questions of the blood
Upon thy blade.　Oh, love me ! love me now,
Mâlmôrda, since thou knowest that the gods
As well as thy strong arms have made me thine
And wholly thine ! '

　　　　　　　" So the days passed in love.
But ugly murmurs were about and rife.
The women crossed themselves as she went by
And shrank from touch of me.　The priests, too, railed
That I was in the witchery of the Galls
Held fast, and had forsworn the great Lord Christ ;
The very bards, who ate my meat and drank
My mead, made laughter of me to my beard,
Playing the ' Fairies' March,' as I strode down
The Hall.
　　　　　　Fair Torcala grieved deep at this,
And bade me tell them she would e'en love Christ
For my sweet sake.　But I who better liked
Her heathen ways, and since I was not learned
In Gospel mysteries, ever put her off.

" One day, Tirdaltha of Clan Mahon, came—
A springald rhymer with a fluting voice
And subtle tongue, who, hearing the loose talk,
Took up its mockery and gave it barbs
Of bitterness in lilting verse. He sang
How late an eagle by a sea-gull charmed
Was turning gull himself, and all the crows—
He meant the priests—were cawing o'er it loud :
But one fell raven, louder still, croaked ' blood,'
And he would win his sea-gull back to sea.

" I came upon him in a grove, where he
Was singing it to full a score of youths
And women, who with white-teethed laughter egged
Him on. They scattered like a flock of crows
Seeing a great kite coming—all but he.
And I, all quivering with so little sting—
Thou knowest how wasp on wasp can madden men—
Laid heavy hand on him while still his thin
Lips parted with the smile of his conceit.
' Thou mock'st the Lady Torcala : defend
Thee quick,' I cried. He muttered something vain :

That he had sung of birds. ' Of birds with beaks
And talons made to tear. Thine eagle is
An eagle still,' I cried.

        " He drew his skein,
And forward set his foot. Well, 't was soon done :
His life went fast upon his song. He fell,
Clutching the earth and striking from his harp
Wild, scattering notes that mocked his mocking song.
Sometimes by night those jangling chords rise yet
Upon mine ear.

        " A message brief I sent
Unto the Mahon that same day that I
Had slain his clansman in hot fight, but held
Me ready, for the love of him and his
Alliance strong, to pay " the price of blood "—
Whatever Brehon law demanded me.
The priests bare home Tirdaltha's corse, and next
Young Cairbre, the slain rhymer's brother, came
To take the gold, a grim and moody boy,
Evil of eye and few of words. I did
Not blame him for his hate of me ; but five

Full days he lingered psalming with the priests,
And with his head upon his hand sat still
And listened to the tale told o'er and o'er
By gossip-mongers. Greediest was he
To hear all ill of Torcala, in which
His pious entertainers did not fail.
When came the day to pay the eric o'er,
He would not enter in the Hall, nor would
He touch or count the gold, but hung the pouch
Wherein 't was stored upon his belt, and went
His way with but one sentence hissing forth :—
' Ask thy wise men, if debt is paid when back
Is brought the gold ? '
                  I answered :—' It is paid
Once and for all when once 't is paid, young sir.'
He lowered his young brows, but said no more.

" The priests then railed the more on Torcala
Until, revolving all, I straight resolved
To seek the hermit bishop out and have
Him wed us. Was I not king—Hy-Cualan's king,
Seed of the mighty Ard Righ, Cahir Mor ?

And should not I as freely choose my queen
As any lout or clod among my clan?
To Glendalough I singly journeyed then,
And lonely mid the mountains o'er the lake
I found the saint at prayer.

       " ' I am Mâlmôrda,
And have come,' I said, ' to bid thee marry me
To Torcala, my spoil won from the Gall.'

" ' Is she a Christian, son ? ' he said all calm.

" ' She shall be, my good lord,' I answered soft.

" ' Is she a maid or widow ? '

                    " ' By my hand,
I care not,' I replied, ' she 's fair and mine.'

" ' Thou carest not ?   Oh, son ! I see confusion
In thine eyes.   She hath a husband, hath she not ? '
' A Pagan dog,' I answered hotly, ' one,
Who ever since I captured his great ship
And her, hangs like a wolf upon our heels,
Harrying the Irish clans around Duv-linn,
Burning Christ's churches, slaying without ruth,
Hoping, no doubt, to make her his again
And win her back, perchance, to paganry.'

" ' Her husband liveth, and it cannot be,'
He answered in low thunder.   ' False art thou
To juggle for me thus this tale of wrong
Upon our church and land, when 't is but lime,

Birdlike, to snare my mind withal, and blur
With pious fraud the promptings of thy lust.'

" Angered, I flushed, but bit my lip and answered:—
'No, no, Lord Bishop ; be my tale o'erwrought
Or no, it is the love as of a star
For star in Heaven, burning but pure, and
If corporeal and consuming, still
Such love as makes the censers of the morn
Fill the rapt air with odors of all flowers
That nod within the dells of Paradise :
A love that knows nor cause nor obstacle,
And would be holy before all men's eyes
As burns it in our hearts and lips and limbs :
A love that 's plighted and returned, with pledge
On pledge of heart 'gainst heart and lip on lip :
A love no prayer can sanctify or seal
More than it is, yet asking that it may
To others be made manifest as 't is
To us, through thee and our Lord Christ.'
                                        ' Her spells

Have meshed thee, man,' he gasped.

'No spells, good priest.
The clowns and harpers and old harridans
So talk ; but 't is not so, thou knowest, if
Thou knowest aught of human joy or dole.'

" 'Thy sin,' he said, ' hath gripped thee by the throat.
The iron neck-ring of thy slavery
Thou takest for a torque of gold.   Our base
Desires are oft our strongest reasoners,
Setting the tongue at service of the eye
That figures roses out of rottenness,
And making man to worship most uncleanly
The filthy clay of which he shapes his god.'

" ' Nay, she is very beautiful, my love,
My Torcala,' I answered him.   ' She is
My lifter-up to great desires, not base.
Would thou hadst seen her, thou hadst loved her
    too.'

" ' Pollution is her name,' he broke in coldly.
'Shear me her red-gold hair ; pluck out her eyes ;
Bring her to me crowned with ashes, barefoot,

Begging humbly for the faith of Christ, and yet
I would not wed thee to her while her lord
Is still alive.'
            My breath came hissing forth ;
My tongue could utter not a sound for rage.
Then went he on.
            ' Thou wouldst not wed her then
Mayhap—a thing unpleasing to thine eyes ;
Thou shudderest at very thought of it.'

" ' Nay,' said I, ' but at picture of so much
Rare beauty brought so low. If thou hadst loved
One woman in thy time, thy sluggish blood,
So tempered by thy wasted hermit life,
Should leap and bubble in thy veins like mine,
At but a tenth part of the desecration
Thou hast dared to mark out for my love ;
Yet if some ruthless demon, Norse or Christian,
Had wrought upon her all the blight thou namest,
She hath my pledge as I have hers, sir priest,
I still would make her mine, as I am king.'

" He crossed himself, and turned from me as I
Were leprous ; then gazing sidewise back, said :—
'' Tis but thy lusting for the heathen's wife
Tuned to her heathen ways ; the very spit
And venom of her trolls made honey-sweet
To lure thee, lip-led, doting into hell.
Her pledge to thee ! What then of her high pledge
To him thou callest wolf, who is her lord ?
E'en as a pagan is she of her false
Gods cursed, and doubly cursed of Him whose law
Says :—Until Death them part, they still are one.'

" ' So then,' I gasped, ' are pagan dogs to have
Thus text and chapter, and the man who wars
On them no prayer save this cold speech of thine ? '

" ' Her husband lives,' he came again with calm,
' And she is not for thee, save to be held
As horse or hound thou takest prize in war :
A shame to thee if thou dost hold her other,
Ay, and a pagan harlot if she yields——'

" He never finished his full speech, for swift
My passion mastered me, and ere I knew,
The rocks were ruddy with his blood. I fled
In horror, for the calm of his old face
Made ice of all my blood that erst was fire.

" Angus, raise not thy hands against me thus
In horror, too.   Older art thou than I ;
Mayhap a score times braver ; but my load
Has been of passion and of grief most heavy.
Some natures there be like to mine which most
In anger rise when man or circumstance
Has touched their weakness or their dearest sin,
And laid it bare—a dire offence to them
In their own love of self—and ere their rage
Thereat turns inward, it may do a deed
Which makes remorse a doubly dreadful fiend,
With newborn crime piled up on olden wrong.
My tears, like drops of blood, heart-wrung, have wet
My cheeks, thinking upon th' unstopped red madness
Of it.   Sacrilege and murder 't was most foul,
But, Angus, when thou deepest damnst it, think

It grew out of a heart made mad with love,
And tortured by blind fools who never knew
The high thoughts that my love made skyward soar,
Scanting the need of sympathy from all
But one.

      The thought that love of one fair work
Of God should make me slayer of a just,
Unpurchased priest who knelt nigh Heaven's gate,
Has wrought me punishment enough in sooth,
Yea, left an aching in my heart that not
The kisses of my Torcala can cure.

" God's grace ! thou weepest for me, Angus ! Nay,
Bow not thy head so on thy hand : the world
Is still before us, urgent, asking us
Account, ay, hour by hour. Watch thou the pass.
See, the sun's round has touched the hills beyond ;
While thus thou gazest let me hurry on.

" None cast the slaying my way ; but his words,
The dead priest's words, were with me night and day ;
And they were true. True, because stronger knit

4

Of human sweet and bitter of the soul
Than e'er command of Patrick or Columba
Out of Holy Writ.   They teach a gospel fierce
By which abides the Ostman heathen, too :—
The man who would, 'fore God and mortal hold
A woman for his own, must have none live
Who can dispute his claim.   I 've seen it clear.
' She is not thine while lives the Ostman,' said
The Priest.   ' She is not thine while I draw breath,'
Saith Asculp.   And say I, ' She is not mine
While Asculp is alive.'   So 't is I 'm here
To stop him and to slay him, and to make
Her mine for aye, or, failing that, to die
By Asculp's blade, none other.

                              " Also this
I have to tell thee, which, untold, no doubt
Has troubled thee, who surely lovest me.
Thou knowest that ere my sire, King Cormac, died
I went a journeying all Erin round
Seeking a noble maiden for a bride,
And how I came back, heart-whole and unwed.

Many I saw whose face and form were dreams
Of loveliness ; but something island-bound
And small of soul there seemed in one and all.
Daughters of war-worn kings, sisters of saints,
They did not please with war songs or with prayers.
Then came I to be king, and still from love
And love-thoughts turned away, and moody grew,
Brea's craggy heights lone haunting to o'erlook
The sea, whose throb and welter took my soul.
There thought I on the glories to be won
Beyond its blue.   I knew it to be shame
That ever we should see the Ostmen come
In might and smite us, and gain foothold strong
In our despite, or if we smote them so
They had to flee, they 'd but to gain the decks
Of their long ships and steal away until
Their gods and their stout rowers sent them back.
I grew to hold it ignominy's brand,
Never to meet them ship to ship, nor in
Stanch vessels hewn from Irish oak to tempt
The tossing waters, making for ourselves
A lordship o'er the sea.   Four cycles gone,

King Niall of the Hostages once led
Ten score of Irish war ships over sea
And ravaged Alba and the Bretan land.
Lives Niall's soul no more ?   Judge, then, the joy
That filled me gazing at fair Torcala,
Thinking that from her loins a mighty race
Of Irish sea-kings should be born whose fame
Would ring the world, joining the Ostman strain
To all the fiercer force in us.   My dream
And hers conjoined.   I was her king
And she the mother of a race to be.
Out of the tempest came she foreordained
My bride.   And if through blood and steel and storm
I won her, now, through steel and blood and death,
At need, I 'll make her mine, so no man's hand
Shall lift and dare deny me.

                              " Do they come ?
I see a new light, Angus, in thy face
That tells of something sterner here than dreams.
Oh, joy to me, I catch a glint of helms,
And now from out the woods they stream in force,

Their spears aslope, their targes careless slung,
As though once nigh the shelter of their rath
That stands there by the sea below, they feared
No Gaelic sword.   I see but one tall steed
And over it the raven banner flies :
Be sure 't is Asculp rides ; and see they bear
Some wounded.   Then, 't is true that they have fought—
No doubt a brush with old Lord Fallan's men.
And they are driving prisoners for their oars ;
God's blood ! they shall not hold them long.   Now
    strain
Thine eyes to see if there be woman's garb
In all their ranks.   Not one.   She 's safe !   Ah, there
I caught a glimpse of long gray beard, red-lit
In sunset as it shone fire-glowing on
The night I won her.   How gloomily he rides,
A great load at his heart that I shall lift.
I catch the jingling of their harness ; see
Their line now shows them black against the sky
That lifts a sea of outspread flame behind them.
With quickening step they 're treading down the hill.
Angus, thy trumpet sound !

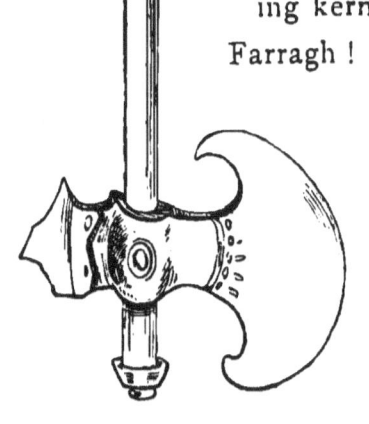

"See their spears lift!

They pause; they turn; now on they
   come; they know

They cannot fight there in the hollow
   vale.

Asculp sees that, and waves them upward
   here.

Too late! They see us and our gallowglasses

Ranging up behind. He hath a war-soul,

Yon gray Dane. He waves his sword
   to charge.

Out from their ambush spring our shout-
   ing kernes.

Farragh! Farragh! they 're on them
      spear and skein,

     Smiting their flank. See their
      shields locked to meet

That onset fierce.

        "Now charge
we in their teeth!

Brave gallowglasses blunt your axes on
The knaves ; Asculp, their captain, is for me—
Never a man to strike him but your Lord !
Into the thick of it ! O God, 't is good
To see your foemen die like stricken wolves,
Snarling and gnashing. Die, accursèd knaves !

" Ho, Asculp ! Asculp ! I am here for thee.
Mâlmôrda calls thee. One of us must die.
For Torcala we fight, that she be mine
Or thine !

                " See him arouse now, and his eyes
Flash fire from under his big brows, his sword
Aloft, his buckler forward borne. Now firm
To earth he springs, his stabbed steed reeling 'neath
    him.
Through clash and press he carves a bloody path.
Masterful thou may'st be, and thy ravens hold
A spell of power ; but greater is the spell
Of Torcala ! Well struck, well clashed, brave Ostman.
Bear thou thus onward to me, smiting all

Before thee down ; I 'm striving ever toward
Thee, too, across thy carrion dogs.   At last !
Now, Asculp, quick ; show fight as thy god Thor
Would have thee fight.   Walhalla waits agape
For thee ! Ha ! I shall show her that brave dint
Upon my shield.   And there ! there ! I said it,
Ostman.   Mine ax has freed thy soul.   Thy ravens
Have thee in their keeping.   *Dhia !* 'T is good
To kill a man who fights and dies like thee,
Old gray-beard sea-dog, and in such a cause ! "

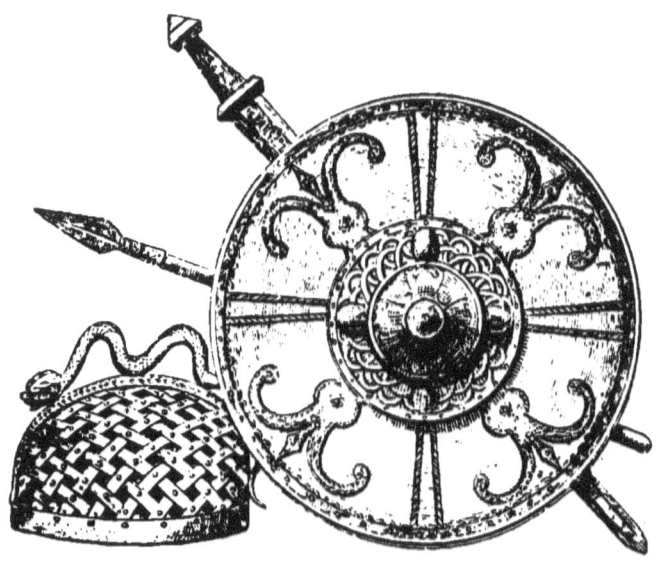

Wild storms the battle 'twixt the mount and sea,
Its fury growing as the shadows fall,
Its red tides pouring as the red sky pales,
Its clamor rising with the deep'ning eve,
As though Death thundering adown the steep
Were racing Night to win a gloomy goal.
Fierce ring the war cries, harsh the dying groans,
While o'er them, through them, sharply sounds
The clatter loud of massy shield on shield,
The crash of axes and the thrust of spears.
Where lies dead Asculp centres now the fray—
A war-god's vortex with the tall straight form
Of young Mâlmôrda at its iron heart,
The waves of slaughter pouring pell-mell in,
Then thrown back broken as in bloody spray.
Brief 't was as fierce ; the Ostmen breaking forth,
To fight not more for victory, but for chance
To flee, and few out leaping the slant whirl
Of Gaelic battle steel.

         Still hovering down
With ever-spreading, ever-nearing wings

Comes darkness, and the horror grows in dying.
The doomed die hard.   The sword blades clash far out,
Where short mad struggles of dim twos and threes
Go scattering, clanging o'er the hillside dun,
Each ending in a groan, a shout and fall.
Now, as of gathering mist, with through it here
And there a sullen star faint glimmering,
A desperate Ostman ten, the last unslain,
Breathless and bloody, form the viking ring—
That ring of steel, where, back to back, shield locked
To shield and bare blades lifted high, the brave
May die hope-lorn, but death is deified.

Around them, as of star-flecked mist, too, four
Dim lines of spearmen close with fore-borne shields.

" Down with your swords, or die ! "

'T is Angus calls.
No answer comes from out the ring of shields.
Then speaks Mâlmôrda, who amid the dead
Still stands on guard by Asculp, seeing all :—
"Hold, clansmen ; Angus, hold ! "

                              The lines, grown tense,
As straining for the charge, relax, and clear
In Ostman tongue rings out :—
                    " I take no prisoners.
Asculp, your Jarl, has fallen by my hand.
I spoil him not.   Throw down your swords, and on
Your shields, brave Ostmen, bear him to Duv-linn.
I have ta'en all that man can take from him.
You have Mâlmôrda's pledge."
                              A bitter laugh
From out the ring of Danes is heard, and one
Voice mutters " Torcala," whereat Mâlmôrda grasps
His ax.   Then rise rough murmurs from the kernes,
Who know not Danish speech, and know not ruth ;
But one stout Dane strides forth and flings his sword
Upon the sward, the others following,
And silent taking rank by two and two,
Uplift old Asculp's body on their shields.
With wondering eyes to thus depart in peace
They pass slow-footed down the hill, the stars
Alone to guide their steps, and from the sea
Below a deep-toned thunder coming faint.

Long stands Mâlmôrda gazing after them,
Until a sudden shout for spoils o'erbears
The clansmen's wonder at this mercy strange,
Ne'er shown before.   Mâlmôrda lifts his hand.
" Bring me the clansmen rescued from the Danes ! "

A silence falls till Angus, by a corse,
Saith :—" Here the last of them to fall lies dead :
The Ostmen slew them as we charged.   Our clansmen
Are they, and of those who stood on watch
Beside the southern portal of the Skealp.
The guard was twenty : here eight men lie dead.
Most like the others lie dead too, beyond
The Skealp—or farther," and he casts a glance
Half anger and half pity at the chief,
As though he would not ruffle further now
A pool of doom whose sombre depths still slept.
But which within the hour would sure reveal
Its ghastliness—how ghastly who could tell ?

A great lump rises in Mâlmôrda's throat.
" And I mayhap have let their slayers go.

I did not write that bloody chapter out
As if I were an Ostman, but made end
In foolish mercy to my foes to suit
The whimsy fancy of my race that dotes
On show." This mutters he, and then aloud :—
" Bring me my horse ! " A swift kerne leads the steed
Up from the wood where long they 'd lain in ambush,
The other clansmen stripping the dead Danes
Of helms and warlike gear. Málmôrda strides
Apart, and glancing down the slope whence passed
The silent bearers of dead Asculp, saith :—
" If thou didst die more for thy love than hate,
Then art thou to be envied of all men.
So would I die, and that I 've spared thy corse
Dishonor, honors me. The Gaelic way
Is better than the Ostman's after all."

He gazes on the sea below that spreads
Its plain of pulsing shadow to the far
Faint promontory lifting up its head
And crowned with stars. He seems to hear the roll
Of waves, and then the woman's image comes

Before his mind, moonlit and beautiful,
Clothed but in jewelled glories of the sea,
And "Torcala," the stars say, " Torcala."
He smiles, then toward the mountains turns, whose slopes
Rise up in frowning purple, pile on pile
Against the sky, save at the pinnacle
Of Golden Spear, on whose sharp crest there gleams
A hue of rose.

" The sun still gilds thy point,
Brave Golden Spear," he cries, " ling'ring to see
Our chastisement upon the Gall."

                " Too long
The sun has set for yon red gleam to come
From him," grim Angus, glooming, answers. " Much
I 've doubted thy rash plan of letting in
The Gall to make assurance thou wouldst kill
Him coming out. That part is done, but how
Has gone the day behind our mountain walls?
Our clan sure met the Ostmen ; but that light
Upon the Golden Spear ? "

               " Victory's lamp ! "
Cries down Mâlmôrda from his prancing steed.
" I ride alone to carry the brave news.
See thou our wounded safe ; our dead to earth,
God rest their souls ! Our clansmen with their spoils
Must at Glen Doon be by the break of day
Or meet the Ostmen here again."

                   " God speed ! "

The clattering hoofs go stamping up the hill,
And Angus, gazing on the Golden Spear,
Sees the rose glow upon it fade, and then
The brighter gleam.
         Mâlmórda riding, thus
Breaks silence in his heart :—
                "Rejoice my soul !
Shadow of night or afterglow is one
To me, for Torcala is won, and no
Gray shadow is between us.   How he fought !
Oh, he had felt her arms about his neck ;
Her red-gold locks had mingled with his beard ;
The lights that make her eyes sea-diamonds twain
Had sent his blood aquiver to his heart.
But she is mine, dead Asculp, she is mine :
Mine is she, good dead priest whose words were true,
God rest thy soul ! and know I dare now look
In thy calm face again, thy bidding done.
As I in soldierwise translated it.

"O brave rock-hearted mountain rising up,
Thy wide-oped jaws crunch only Erin's foes !

To-night thou ope'st the way to love for me.
Thy tumbled bowlders are as roses soft
On beds of tender moss laid, like her bow'r,
Where safe and longing she awaits my kiss,
Low list'ning for the tramping of my steed.

" Into the pass, then, steed.   'Tis dark : but stars
Are clearer seen the deeper lies the road.
Nearer to thee, my love, and nearer still !

" O jagged rocks, gray granite sentinels,
Ye wondered that the Danes passed by unhurt
To-day.   Lo, here 's their captain's blood upon
My blade : ay, Asculp's blood.   I give it thee.
See as I gallop by the brook I lean
Me down and wash it off.   O Torcala,
His blood 's no more between us.   Nothing now
But clear, fair ways for love, a heaven-song,
Long days of merry life, long eves of love,
An Erin growing grand and strong in men
And ships, and thou, the Stranger Queen, t' outshine
The glories of Queen Meve ! "

5

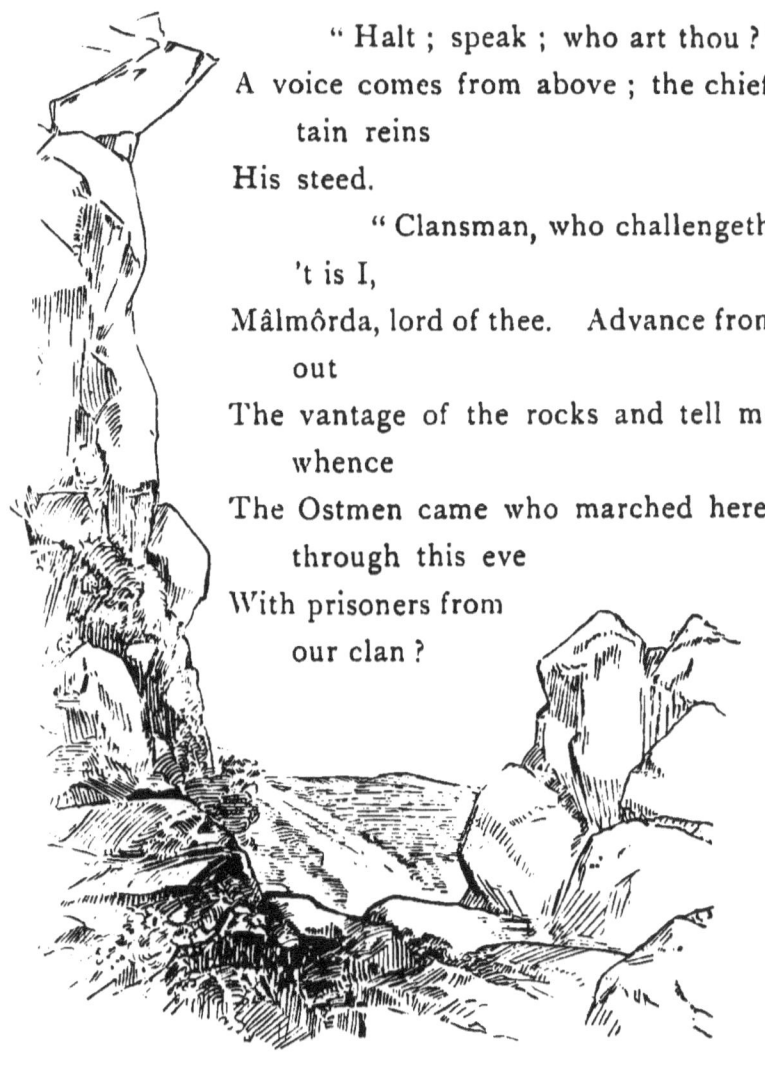

"Halt ; speak ; who art thou ?"
A voice comes from above ; the chieftain reins
His steed.
            "Clansman, who challengeth,
   't is I,
Mâlmôrda, lord of thee.   Advance from
   out
The vantage of the rocks and tell me
   whence
The Ostmen came who marched here-
   through this eve
With prisoners from
   our clan ?

" Why speak'st thou not ?
I am thy king, Mâlmôrda ; tell me straight
Whence came the Danes, from Dair Glenn or the West ?

" No word.   Surely I heard a voice but now
Call halting me.   The knave 's afeard.   I hear
His footsteps up the rocks ; the loose stones drop
As hastes he on.   Ha, fool ! he dreads lest I
Should hold him to account that he did not
Lone-handed stop the Ostmen !
                                        Rascal !   Ho !
I do not take thee for great Fionn, he
Who clove the hills in sunder !
                                        On good steed !
God's wounds !   That sound of woe, that from the height
Comes in long ululation, I like not.
Belike the fleeing sentinel now thinks
Our force was slaughtered all on Ostman ground,
And I alone escaped.   That angers me.
He should have known his king, Mâlmôrda, better.
God ! were that so, and had the Danes prevailed
My corse had lain among my men.   Ho, Ho !

Mayhap the knave thinks 't is Mâlmôrda's ghost,
And would not, on his life, change speech with me.
'T is strange to fear the dead ; they are not grim
To me.
   The path 's not wide : go surely, horse,
If slow. The vale once opened thou shalt shake
Thy black mane on the wind. Tread sure, good steed."

" Woe ! Woe ! Mâlmôrda ! "

      " Shrills that cry once more !
I mock thy banshee wail, false caitiff kerne,
Who seem'st to stride along the cliff above
As making sure I 'd hear thee. Spare thy breath !
The Danes lie dead between the mount and sea !
What else is there to reck since they are dead ?

" Silence again ! 'T is better, for 't is dark
Down here, and one must ride eyes fixed on earth,
Not gazing up at thee. These upstart rocks,
Like granite Asculps, bar my way. O dead,
Stout fighter and strong lover, grand if gray,

The wife thou hadst is mine ! My dream, my hope
Stand realized. Queen of the sept Hy-Cualan,
Bride of Mâlmórda is thy Torcala !
The Ostman skill and suppleness once wed
With Irish strain, our royal race shall feel
Emprise dreamed not by Ostman or by Gael.
Mistress of sea and shore as of the crag
And lawn shall Erin be, and those who long
For flowering lives shall not be forced to choose
'Twixt saint and soldier. Yea, our ranting bards
Shall have high songs to sing, whereto their harps
Can make the music of the morn vibrate,
Ay, and these hot invaders who now come
In thunder, and steal out on sliding keels—
As glide their vikings over icy fields
Where North and Night are one—shall be our
    friends.
In every vale a Torcala shall reign,
And Ostmen shall come asking us for wives
Of Gaelic blood, until our mingled race
Shall rule the world. This thy revenge shall be,
Gray Asculp.

Hark, what raven croaks by night ?
Dark as their feathers be, they fly by day.
Nay, stumble not, good steed, if I but slip
The rein to gaze up at the stars above.
Yea, a whole flight of ravens wide of wing,
Circling and darting to and fro. Why flies
The Ostman bird by night? Ho, Valkyrs they,
Back flying sure from bearing Asculp's soul
To Odin's bosom, ere his Danes have borne
His body to Duv-linn ! Fly, ravens, fly !
Ha, there darts by an Irish kite ascream !
He circles and comes fluttering down. What, dead ?
No ! Heaven of Patrick or Walhall of Dane,
I take no omens from ye ! Asculp is dead,
And his three hundred with him all but ten !
These ten I spared to bear their dead jarl home.

"On, on, good horse ! more open now the path.
They did not dare, three hundred strong, to force
Glen Doon, and tempt death 'fore Mâlmôrda's rath,
No, no ; as stole they in this morn from Brea
Old Fallan's kernes of Fercualan rose up

And smote them, and by Dair Glen drove them home,
And here below they fell in fleeing on
My mountain guard and killed or captured them.
That must be how it happed. No Ostman dog
Could know the westward track to that fair nest
Where in these summer eves my love was fain
To rest within my arms. But Gaelic wood-craft,
Long foretaught, could find the path that leads up
To the crest of Moyla's Hill where Torcala
Awaits me—where the moon on rising meets
Her moon-sweet eyes adream. She little counts
What news I have for her. May I not toy
With it awhile and tent her till she craves
To know why I went fighting forth, and told
Her naught, my purpose or my hope? But she
Will guess full soon what makes the blaze within
Mine eyes, the laughter in my heart. She 'll guess
That Asculp 's dead and she Mâlmôrda's queen.
Now, now the rocks and cliffs roll back, and wide
The plain spreads out. Extend thee, horse ; thy feet
Must bear me swifter, swifter on to love.
The Golden Spear before me towering up !

What glow is that which lights thy west slope all
From base to pointed crest ?

                    Thou lookest straight,
Old Irish mount, atoward green Moyla's Hill
Where Torcala is waiting.   Answer me,
And shame these Ostman ravens, Whence thy light ?

" Ah, the glow brightens : now it darkles down.
A signal fire on Moyla's Hill, I ween
It is.   The Norse child knows that Erin's gods
Of old loved leaping, laughing, shooting flame.

" Down the broad slope past Daira's woods and then
To breast the westward upland, and we 'll see
The hill-top rise beyond.   One glance will tell
Us all.   On, on !   My soul has caught the flame :
Wide nostrils and quick pattering hoofs, the word.

" *Well thou answerest, steed ; well thou answerest !*
Keeping time to thy hoof beats my heart beats,
Tramping louder as faster the sparks fly,
Gallop on like a Valkyr, still gallop on.
Hollow thunder thou mak'st on the turf-land ;

As a javelin we speed by the timber ;
In the open thy hoof-tramps beat louder,
While the dust rises up to the smoke-cloud.
Eager, oh, eager my soul and my stallion ;
Touch but the earth as thou spurn'st it, uplifting ;
In the heart of thy rider such speeding
And striding and reaching, that never yet
Steed for his master could tramp on as fast
As the hurricane wild of desire sweeps him
Onward, enwrapping him, urging him on
To where, leaping and roaring, flame-welcome
Waits him—the fire of my love or the torch
Of disaster. To the fire ! To the flame !
Oh, gallantly, valiantly thunderest thou.
Fast are we rising ; the shadows grow thin.
Twenty strides and we 'll gaze on Moyla's Hill,
Whence comes the hot breath of the stifling wind.
Now, slower, good steed.

             Gods ! 't is no signal fire ;
Too great the blaze. It has outleaped their care,
And wraps the woodland wide ! No sign of life
But frighted birds and wild things rushing forth.

" To me ! to me, Mâlmôrda !

      To that cry
That should have started up a score of kernes,
No answer comes, no trumpet blast replies.
Could the rank priests have risen up and led
The scoffers on to fire her bow'r while I
Was smiting Asculp ? 'T is most like, else now
Would some be here in sight to watch for me.
If they but dreamed 't was I that slew the saint
They 'd do 't, for though they honor martyrs' bones
They hate the martyr-makers. They are that
Much men like others, but they would not dare
To harm a hair of hers ; they 're that much human.

"Vain guess ! To know it all we must quick on.
Fail me not now, my steed ; I 'm needed there.
Straight for the flames we 'll ride.

       Across the path
The blazes leap. Swerve not ! Thou fear'st not fire :
Thou bearest it in bearing me. The hot
Black smoke, the sparks that show'r, the roaring flames
Are not more terrible than I.

No, no
We cannot face that hell of flame. We must
Bear windward, fronting it. Yes, the dark path
That winds up by the northern slope must yet
Be safe. See the great blackened trunks fall prone,
Each sending up more sparks than there are stars.

"Stars ! the sweet eyes of Torcala ! stars ! stars !

"Now upward ; thou hast nobly done, good horse,
'T will widen soon : see there an open space.
Oh, stagger not. On, on !
                        Why halt'st thou now,
Snorting in fright, mane-lifted, throwing back,
Thou who dared'st fire ? At thy feet a corse !
To earth !
            Ha, fleest thou to the fire, poor steed,
Rather than stay by me ? Yet fear I not ;
Mâlmôrda 's equal to his fate alone.

"Whose corse ? Surely I know that boyish face.
Now, by St. Coll, 't is Cairbre of Clan Mahon,

Brother of young Tirdaltha, whom I slew
For mockery of Torcala. He bore
The eric that I paid for that hot deed.
Well I remember him. Who slew the boy?
Must all my sins come trooping here for judgment?
At his girdle hangs a treasure. Gold! Gold!
The pouch I gave him, and he bore it back
In token that he sought revenge. He has
Found death instead!

              Treason! Upon the mound
A score of corses mingled, kernes and Danes!
Young Cairbre led old Asculp here! Now out,
My skein, and on, Mâlmôrda, on! No hand
But thine can cut the web that holds thee fast.

"At every step a corse; there three! Her bower
Unroofed—a skeleton in black. They found
Her not. He did not get her, that I know,
Else he had carried her in triumph home.
She 's safe. My clansmen fought him, and he left
His dead behind him as they fell, which marks
His haste in going—grim, baffled war-dog!

What matter so she 's safe ?   Clan, land and all
In fire, if she but rises up and greets me !

" I do not find her, though around her bower,
I search, heart-leaping, fearing every corse
Be hers.
      The fight went this way up, still up,
A bitter fight, up to the topmost rock.
This pile of dead close-locked !   Over their faces
Must I stride.   There, there in the firelight full,
Above them all, her robe !   ' T is she !   O God !
Her face so white, her staring eyes !   Torcala !
Mâlmôrda calls thee.   Torcala !   White Angel,
Hear me !   O Torcala !   Dead !   Dead among dead !
O hell-sent furies, ravening bloody dogs,
Would ye again had breath that I again
Might slay ye still more bloodily !   My heart,
My heart !   Would that their spears had pierced it ere
It strangled in this suffocating pain !
Torcala, I come to thee !   Oh, for one
Heart-beat hear me !
           Did her eyes move ?   Did a smile

Flit o'er her face ?   Closer !   I saw 't but now.
Madness !   'T is but the shadows flickering
In the flames.   O Torcala !   Torcala !
Gone, gone from me !

                    Thy hand cold, and thy brow.
Thy heart ?   Ah, there an Ostman dagger 's plunged.
Asculp's !   His wingéd raven for a hilt.
Out tool, hell-forged, and rust in Irish earth ;
Thou 'lt blight forever him who touches thee.
The hand that drave thee soon grew weak and white,
And I am marked for doom who plucked thee forth.
That little matters now.   There 's none to kill,
And none to love in all the world for me ;
Yea, none to hate—I who have killed and loved
Unto the fill.   That blinds and crushes me.
Why kneel I here, and grope around and touch
Her death-cold form ?   Is there naught else to do ?
To have fought hard and ridden hot-foot here ;
Joy, hope, and fever, fury all brought short
To end.   Out of a world-quake nothing comes.
I cannot give it name, this numb standstill
That robs my grief of tears, and horror that

Should master me and stir to livid rage
Finds me here prostrate and unmoved if all
The world should end.
                        She must not thus aheap
Lie as she fell.   The gold band rolls but now
From off her red-gold hair as I uplift
Her head. My hand 't was placed it there this morn.
Oh, God be thanked, I feel the horror sting.
Lie pillowed here a minute's space, fair head,
Ere once for all I lay thee back on earth.
Dead, dead, O Torcala, my Torcala !

" My tears fall rainlike now ; they should be fire
To match my sorrow that consumes my life.
How my breath comes and goes in gushes ! Heart,
All is awry, and nothing to be set
In place. What I set out to do to free
Our lives I did. It proved a vengeance wreaked
By gods through me, yet letting me not know
'T was vengeance ; for when I fought and slew him,
'T was in joy tumultuous and in hope,
No edge of cutting hatred in it all.

I dreamed myself a sacrificer, not
An executioner.   Heaven has mocked me—
—Thy heaven, love, and mine, my God and thine.
They leave me none to slay when most my brain
Cries, Kill.
    Ah, thought that makes my heart leap up!
I still do live.   Here, skein of mine, is work
And sheathing for thee in a bitter heart !
I stand erect and look at heaven now.

"Ay, roll ye this way, flames and stifling smoke !
Blow this way, furnace wind !   Here came the Dane
That loosed ye ; Why not ye ? I still can see
The stars up through the drifting smoke, and there
I 'll join thee, Torcala.
    Strange phantasms grow.
There, in the lowering smoke-cloud, see I clear
The calm face of the priest I slew look down ;
Nor does it chide.   Tell me, good priest, what god
Has claimed her—Asculp's angry god or thine?
Gone in the whirling cloud, and gave no sign.
Ah me, I know not where to seek her soul !

" Gray Asculp was the first to follow her.
He heard the priest's words in his heart and came
And owned her long enough to strike his blade
Into her breast, so none could hold her more.
Ostman, dead Ostman, she is thine, and I
Am food for Norseland's ravens ! Priest, calm priest
Thy words are true—' to hold is not to have,'
My skein shall write them deep upon my heart !

" Stream up, ye flames, whose tongues lick up the live,
And leave it dead ! Death has been here before you.
Naught of green luscious life you 'll find ; but husks,
The souls all gone—one lovely corse, and one
Whose soul had lofty dreams ; who sets him free
By one stroke of a blade.
       Set free ? Then she
Too has the freedom of the stars. My love,
The vasts of space shall not bar me from thee,
Art thou not hovering in the deep blue calm
Above the fire—a lone star among stars—
Eager awaiting me ? I come.
        'T is done !

O skein, thou hast cut all my doubt away?
O love, who died'st for me, I die for thee
As Asculp died!

     He cannot share that kiss,
There, there upon thy brow, love, Torcala!"

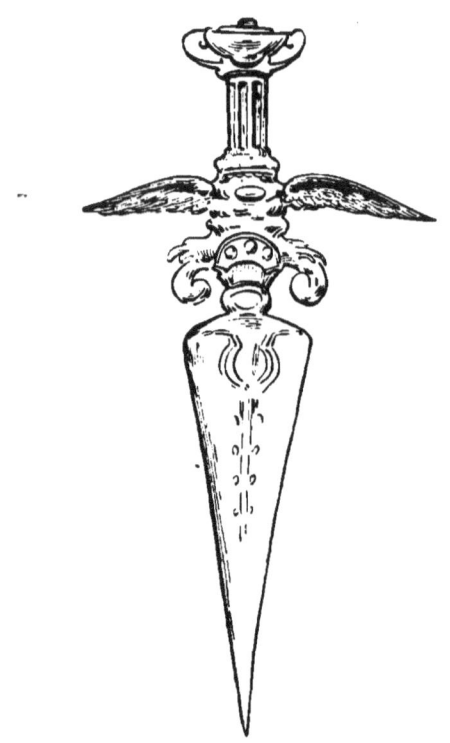

NOTES.

" *The land they called the Blest*," Fore-song, p. 2.

Ireland was so called after the conversion of the Irish to Christianity by St. Patrick, in the fifth century, because of the blessings pronounced upon it by the saint, and because of the great piety of the people. Never was a religion, once seized, more ardently embraced. Centres of devotion and seats of learning sprang up on every side. Its saints and recluses, living saintly lives, became innumerable, and it was known at Rome as the Holy Island, the Blessed Island, the Island of Saints.

Of the many ancient names of Ireland, the historian Keating recalls Inis-na-Veevah—the Isle of Woods ; Creea-na-vunnaya—the Far-Off Land ; Inis Elga—the Noble Island. Eri, Fola, and Banba are three names successively given to Ireland by ancient native poets, being the names of three queens of the race of Tuatha-De-Dananns, from the first of which the name Erin is easily derived. Inis-Fail—the Island of Destiny—is another poetic name. Muy-Inis—the Island of Mists—is probably poetic also, but surely descriptive. It was also widely known as Scotia, a name derived, it is said, from Scota, the wife of Milesius, and of Egyptian origin ; it was the name most used by the later Latin and early Christian writers. The native Irish called themselves Scots in their own tongue. Hibernia, the most usual and most ancient Latin name, was derived from the race of Eber, one of the children of Milesius, and therefore of Spanish or Iberian origin. Juverna, the name given to the island by Ptolemy, is evidently a mutation of Hibernia. Irlanda, whence the modern English name, Ireland, is derived, was the name by which it was known to the Scandinavians and Saxons. This may be also a derivative of Eri—as Eri-landa, but, as O'Mahony observes, "the tribe of Ir anciently ruled the north-east of Ireland, and came first into contact with the Gothic nations, and it is probable that Ireland owes the foreign title ' Irlanda ' to the Irians of Ulster, as it may, perhaps, that of Hibernia to the Iberians or tribe of Eber of Munster."

" Hold not the Ostmen lordship," page 7.

The events of the poem take place toward the end of the first half of the ninth century, when Maelsaechlain, or Malachy, was Ard Righ or high king of Ireland.

The Scandinavian kingdom of Dublin had just been founded. During the previous forty years many descents had been made upon the Irish coast by the Norwegian and Danish sea-rovers, and Dublin, or, as it was known to the Irish, Dubhlinn Bally ath Cliath [literally, Black-pool of the town of Hurdleford], was taken in force, and occupied in 838 A.D. by the invaders. It was at once fortified, and became for them an abiding foothold in Ireland. It gradually grew in importance as a settlement and as a stronghold. The merely predatory incursions of the first-comers gave place to a fixed colonization. It became a trading-port for their sea-going merchants, as well as a place for the sale of plunder gathered elsewhere. The fugitive records of the time give glimpses of almost continuous wars between the invaders and the Irish tribes around them. Dublin was besieged and taken by Irish armies more than once, but fresh viking hordes soon returned in large fleets, and retook the city. Wars between the invaders themselves occurred frequently in the ninth century, the presence of a hostile fleet in Dublin Bay being the first sign that the supremacy of those Scandinavians already in possession was to be bloodily tested.

At times the newcomers and the old united in a foray upon the inland kingdoms, the churches and holy shrines being repeatedly despoiled and great slaughter done. Hardy, subtle, and fearless as were these pagans from the north, they failed to consolidate their conquests far from the blue water where they were at home. Every harbor in Ireland of any consequence had its Danish settlement held by force of arms, but except for brief periods and in different portions at a time, did they hold sway over the inland territories, even when so broad a river as the Shannon invited them into the heart of the country. The tenacity of the Irish tribes in fighting for their homes, shrines, and herds, accounts largely for this failure, but the disposition of the vikings to regard the civilized world simply as their prey had its share in telling against the permanence of most of their conquests.

In Dublin, or Dyflin, as the Scandinavian records call it. the conditions were more favorable for a permanent hold, and for two centuries the Scandinavian kingdom of Dublin was in existence. Its boundaries were not very definite, or at least were subject to frequent change. It certainly extended at all times from Bray Head to Howth, and as far inland as Clondalkin, but generally farther north into Meath and farther south into Wicklow.

According to an ancient Gaelic manuscript of the 11th century entitled, *The Wars of the Gaedhil with the Gaill*, the first invasion of the foreigners took place in 812 A.D., but other authorities place it as far back as 794 A.D. Probably the invasion noted in the manuscript was the first descent in overwhelming force and marked by great and continued disasters to the Irish. The fleet of the foreigners was one hundred and twenty ships—probably a fighting force of eight thou-

sand men. Another fleet is noted in 834. In 839 there came a " Great
Royal Fleet into the North of Erinn " under Turgeis, whom Professor
Boyesen identifies as Thorgisl.   After several bloody battles, he
extended his sway over the northern half of Ireland, but his rule only
lasted thirteen years.   He was killed and his followers were driven to
the sea.   The first invasion of " Dublin of Ath Cliath," noted in this
M.S. was by an Ostman fleet of sixty-five ships in 838, but there is
reason to assert that the Fingall, or white strangers, had long before
made trading settlements there, and that this invasion was but one of
those where a new horde was added to the old invaders, now fortressed
settlers and traders as well as a garrison.   How partial a list of the
Ostmen's piratical descents the foregoing must be, may be gathered
from the statement :—" After this came great sea-cast floods of
foreigners into Erinn, so that there was not a point thereof without a
fleet."   The progress and sway of these invading swarms were hotly
disputed, and so widespread were the disasters of the Irish and so
frequent the battles fought that we may well believe this old chroni-
cler who so naively writes :—" Much, indeed, of evil and distress
did they [the invaders] receive, and much was received from them
which is not recorded at all."   Until 876 these swarms continued to
pour in.   By this time the Ostman settlements were strongly grounded
at every port and estuary of any consequence in Ireland, and a cessa-
tion of the invasions followed for forty years.   The Irish seaport
towns had become points from which fleets of the Ostmen started to
help their predatory brethren on the Rhine, in France, in Brittany,
and other parts of the continent of Europe as well as Great Britain—
where, too, the prospect of plunder was greater.

Some amalgamation followed between the Ostmen and the native
Irish after the former had been Christianized in the early part of the
tenth century ; but it was confined to a few tribes or septs, and was

individual rather than communal, for the lines remained distinctly drawn to the end.

The end came with the great battle of Clontarf, fought on Good Friday, 1014 A.D., between the Irish under King Brian Boru and the Danes of Dublin to whose assistance Ostmen from Scotland, England, Brittany, and Norway had flocked in immense fleets. Some Irish tribes of Leinster fought on the side of the Danes. It was a battle to the death, and the Irish won. The Ostman power was broken. The Kingdom of Dublin had rulers with Ostman names for a century after, and the Ostmen merchants and traders remained, but the glory of the sea-rover departed from them thereafter.

" *From Brea unto Ben Edar*," page 7.

The great headlands of Howth (Ben Edar) and Bray Head (Brea).

" *Quick to strike these Danes*," page 8.

The viking invaders from Norway and Denmark were at first called simply " Galls " or foreigners, by the Irish. Later they were distinguished as Finn-gall (white strangers) or Dubh-gall (black strangers). The distinction is believed to have been founded on the white shields of the former and the black shields of the latter, who are subsequently called Danes, implying that the " white strangers " were from Norway. Lochlannagh was another name applied to the first invaders. It has been held to mean the Lakelanders, or people from the land of the lakes or fiords, but doubt is thrown on this derivation. As " Ostmen "—men from the East—the Scandinavian invaders of Ireland were first known to the English-speaking people—a list of the " Ostmen kings " of Dublin being made for Henry II. shortly after the conquest of the eastern portion of Ireland, under Strongbow.

" *Young Málmórda of Hy-Cualan, king,*" page 8.

Written in Gaelic the name is ᚋᚐᚑᛁᛘᚑᚱᚆᚐ—indicating a fine fulness of sound. It signifies the proud champion—from " Mordha " proud, and " Maol " tonsured—as priests are—the servants and champions of Christ. The name occurs frequently in the genealogies of the noble and royal families descended from the Brann, whose abode was in Leinster, and whose territories were those of Hy-Cualan and Hy-Faelin—portions of the present countries of Wicklow and Kildare. It is on the debatable ground between Hy-Cualan and the Ostman territory and overlooking Dublin Bay that the opening scenes of the poem are laid.

" *Torcala,*" page 11.

The name under the early Norse form of Torkathla is met with in the sagas. It is a derivative of Thor—the Norse war-god—feminized. Torkall and Torcull are men's names from the same source.

" *Sitric's mighty fleet,*" page 13.

Some idea of the numbers, organization, manning, working, and fighting of these viking fleets can be gained from a reading of the sagas. Du Chaillu's great work, *The Viking Age*, is an encyclopedia of the subject—their long ships, dragon ships, and all kinds of fighting craft.

" *Above Delginis,*" page 15.

The Gaelic name of Dalkey Island. The Irish word means Thorn (Delg) Island (Inis). The name received its present form from the Ostmen who substituted the Norse word " ey," island for " inis." Its importance was recognized in very early times, it having been fortified by the earliest Irish tribes. The Ostmen fortified it in turn, the Sound which lies between it and the mainland affording fine anchorage. Hence many of the fleets harbored there.

" *The Valkyrs*," page 16.

The raven maidens, choosers of the slain in the Norse mythology, who bore the souls of dead warriors to Walhalla, the home of Odin, father of the gods. There the warriors feasted, fought, and slew each other day after day, ever reviving at evening.

" *Leinen's Hill*," page 19.

The Hill f Killiney—in Gaelic, " Cill-Inghen-Leinen "—the church of Leinen's daughters. The church was destroyed by the Danes. A superb view of Dublin Bay and the Dublin and Wicklow mountains is obtainable from Killiney Hill.

" *Through the Skealp*," page 23.

The Scalp, a well-known mountain chasm or cleft in the outward range of the Wicklow mountains. The word "skealp" or "scelp" means something cut off by a knife or hatchet, and here refers to the legend of the mountain having been cloven in twain by Fionn, the greatest of Ireland's legendary heroes—at once the Gaelic Herakles and Achilles. This pass forms a narrow defile, with lofty shelving ramparts on each side, from which large masses of granite have fallen ; masses of detached rock are heaped together in the wildest confusion above the road, apparently about to topple down. It is very wild and gloomy. During the Danish occupation, and for centuries after the English invasion, it was a veritable fortress for the clans of O'Byrne and O'Tuathal. It was never taken in front. A stream winds at the bottom of it.

"*By Fercualan,*" page 24.

A northern Wicklow district near the sea-shore and south of the Dublin line.

"*The Norns were by,*" page 31.

The Norns were the three Fates or Parcae of the Northern nations. See the Eddas.

"*His berserks,*" page 37.

The chosen warriors or champions who fought in the stem or prow of the viking ships.

"*The very bards,*" page 38.

Every king and chieftain had his bards, who played upon the harp and composed and sang inflated songs in praise of the king and his ancestors, or in denunciation of his enemies. They had many privileges, and often abused them. At one time they grew so numerous and so exacting, that they were suppressed for a number of years.

"*The price of blood,*" page 40.

Under the Brehon law, which was supreme in Ireland, the relatives of a man slain had a right to exact an eric or fine from his slayer—the amount being decided by the Brehons or judges.

"*The hermit bishop,*" page 41.

From the close of the sixth century, Glendalough—the valley of the lakes—in Wicklow, was famous for its monastic establishment, founded by St. Kevin, its first bishop. Following his example, many priests and prelates in succeeding centuries secluded themselves absolutely from the world, in caves and rude huts around the lakes. The churches and monastery were burned time and again by the Danes. The ruins and round-tower still remaining are most instructive relics of early Irish ecclesiastical architecture. St. Kevin was the patron saint of the Branndaigh, or, as they were later known, the O'Byrnes.

" *Ard Righ, Cahir Mor,*" page 41.

Cahir Mor, or Cahir the Great, was supreme monarch of Ireland in the second century. From him a great number of the Southern Gaelic families trace their descent—the Branndaigh, lords of Hy-Cualan among them.

" *A torque of gold,*" page 45.

The neckring, often of pure gold and fine workmanship, worn by chieftains in this age, and notably by the leaders of the vikings.

" *Venom of her trolls,*" page 47.

The trolls were the Norse fairy witches : they wrought ill to men by drawing them into all sorts of snares, and were endowed with supernatural powers.

" *Niall of the Hostages,*" page 52.

Among the captives brought back to Ireland in the beginning of the fifth century, from one of the King Niall's piratical descents upon the coast of Brittany, is said to have been St. Patrick, then a godly youth of sixteen. Escaped from slavery in Ireland, he repaid his debt to the country by becoming its apostle.

"*The viking ring*," page 58.

In the sagas it is described as the "viking burgh," or fortress. The warriors were pledged so to gather to the last around their king or standard when hard pressed in battle, and it was a point of the highest honor never to break the burgh, but by falling dead in arms.

"*The pinnacle of Golden Spear*," page 62.

The Golden Spears was the fine figurative name given by the ancient Irish to the two cone-shaped mountains in Northern Wicklow, now vulgarly called the Great and Little Sugar Loaf. The crest of the Great Sugar Loaf, towering above the neighboring mountains, catches the last rays of the sun upon its white point, and so shines as a veritable Golden Spear above the darkening land. This mountain seems by day to bar the southern end of the Scalp, but its base is several miles from the mouth of that sombre pass.

THE NEW YORK MAIL AND EXPRESS.

The story of an insurrection which is hopeless, viewed from the political side, gives for that very reason perhaps a better canvass for the picture of a young hero who stakes his life in his country's cause when the very decrees of destiny are against success. This picture the author puts before us with a direct simplicity that is the best effect of art. His Emmet is a man with whom his country's honor is even more a primary purpose than her independence; and who never hesitates to believe that it is better for a people to perish in the battle for liberty than to live without it. The character of Miss Curran is even with the noble delicacy of the lines drawn by Washington Irving, and more could scarcely be said for it. It is a characteristic hint of the ways of fate happily worked into the drama, that while the hero's life is forfeited for what he has done in the cause of his country, it is in the effort to see his lady love that he loses it. In the last act of this tragedy the highest note of human passion—the lover's farewell at the foot of the gallows, on which he is to die for his country—is very finely and beautifully touched. At this place there might be for an author, less filled with the artistic sense of the modesty of nature, a terrible temptation to write rant; but we have here a fine literary realization of the best conception of such a scene.

NEW YORK HERALD.

The story of Emmet is followed faithfully, and there could not be a gentler type of fair and pure womanhood than Sarah Curran. Emmet himself is rather an ideal impersonation of the Irish hope of independence, and as we read his speeches, with their eloquence and courage, we feel as if they were a protest and a prayer. As a work of art Mr. Clarke's tragedy is of high order. The scenes are concise, definitive, the plot moving to its purpose with Greek simplicity and directness.

Mr. Clarke has written an honest, powerful tragedy which will hold a high place in dramatic literature.

THE PHILADELPHIA TIMES.

In " Robert Emmet—A Tragedy of Irish History " (G. P. Putnam's Sons), by Joseph I. C. Clarke, our literature is enriched with the best play in prose ever written and printed in America. Simple in language, direct in narration and masterly in arrangement, Mr. Clarke's play can scarcely fail to act as well as it reads, and it reads like a romance. The casual reader, who may chance to take it up, will find it impossible to lay it down until he has finished the absorbing story.

CHRISTIAN AT WORK.

Interwoven with the story of his pure patriotism is that of a love so true and touching that all the higher dramatic elements are present, awaiting only the hand of art to arrange them. This Mr. Clarke has done most successfully in his tragedy.

NEW YORK TIMES.

The parting scene in jail and the court scene, when Emmet makes his historic address to the judge, are managed with power, and are most moving to the reader.

TRUTH.

It is the only work upon that hero which rises to the height of his own deeds. The diction is pure and elevated, the scenes dramatic and effective, while the simple pathos of the work will appeal to every reader, whatever may be his political opinions.